BS 3.79

DO YOU KNOW COLORS?

A Random House PICTUREBACK®

DO YOU KNOW COLORS?

by J.P. Miller and Katherine Howard

RANDOM HOUSE 🏠 NEW YORK

Copyright © 1978 by Random House, Inc. All rights reserved under International and Pan-American Copyright Conventions. Published in the United States by Random House, Inc., New York, and simultaneously in Canada by Random House of Canada Limited, Toronto.

Library of Congress Cataloging in Publication Data: Miller, John Parr. Do you know colors? SUMMARY: Reveals how some colors are made from blending others and depicts objects in each color. 1. Color—Juvenile literature. [1. Colors] I. Howard, Katherine, Joint author. II. Title. QC495.5.M54 535.6 78-1133 ISBN: 0-394-83956-0 (B.C.); 0-394-83957-9 (trade); 0-394-93957-3 (lib. bdg.). Manufactured in the United States of America. A B C D E F G H I J   1 2 3 4 5 6 7 8 9 0

RED

This color is red. My hat is red. The cardinals are red. Do you know what else is red?

POINSETTIA

MOUN
ASH B

CARDINAL

HOLLY

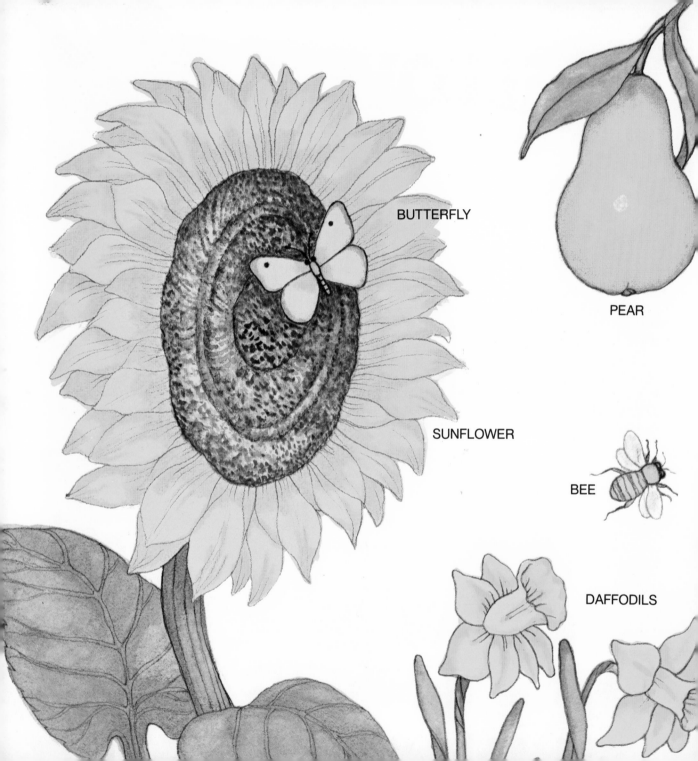

BUTTERFLY

PEAR

SUNFLOWER

BEE

DAFFODILS

YELLOW

LEMONS

Yellow is the color of these flowers — sunflowers, daffodils, and dandelions. How many yellow things can you find?

CANARY

DANDELIONS

BUTTERCUPS

BLUE JAY

BLUE SPRUCE

BLUEBERRIES

BLUEBELLS

BLUE

This color is blue.
The blue jay is blue.
The water is blue, too.

DRAGONFLY

IRIS

MORNING-GLORIES

ORANGE

Red and yellow make orange.
Some butterflies and autumn leaves
are orange like this fox.

TIGER LILY

LADYBUG

AUTUMN LEAVES

NEWT

MONARCH BUTTERFLY

FOX

INCHWORM

GREEN

GREEN FLY

FROG

I mix blue and yellow together to make the color green. How many green things do you see?

TURTLE

LILY PAD

KATYDID

PRAYING MANTIS

LEAF

GRASS

GREEN SNAKE

PURPLE

PANSY

Red and blue make purple.
Grapes and plums are purple.
Have you ever seen a purple
monster?

VIOLETS

PURPLE GALLINULE

PLUMS

PURPLE MONSTER

GRAPES

THISTLE

BLACK

Some ants are black. Some berries are black. There's a blackbird in the black bear's blackberry pie!

BLACKBIRD

BLACKBERRIES

ELDERBERRIES

BLACK BEAR

ANTS

WHITE

ROOSTER

I am painting the brown fence white.
The snowman is white. Do you know
these white animals?

SNOWY OWL

ERMINE

DUCKS

SNOWMAN

SNOWSHOE HARE

FIELD MOUSE

BROWN

Brown is red and yellow and blue
and black all mixed together.

MOTH

RABBIT

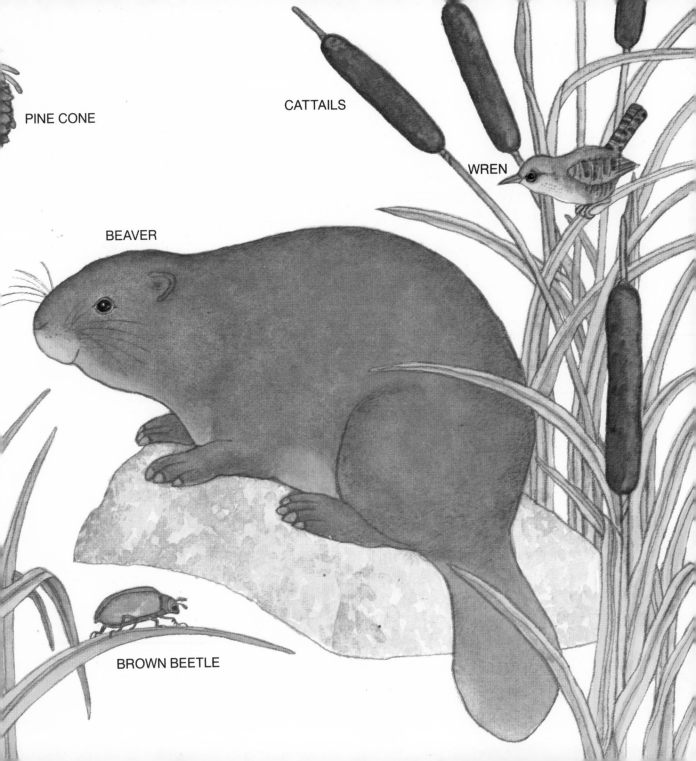

PINE CONE

CATTAILS

WREN

BEAVER

BROWN BEETLE

PINK

White and red make pink.
Flamingos are pink.
There's a pink pig
in the clover patch.

ROSE

PIG

CLOVER

FLAMINGO

CARNATION

TONGUE

GRAY

White and black make gray.
Some of the biggest animals are gray.
Some little ones are gray, too.

RHINOCEROS

LIZARD

ROCK

PEBBLES

ELEPHANT

TAN

This color is tan.
White and brown make tan.
How many tan things can you find?

HOUND

SANDPIPER EGGS

SAND

SANDPIPERS

PALOMINO PONY

SNAIL

CAT

OLIVE

OLIVES

UNIFORM

I mix green and yellow and brown to make the color olive. The soldier's uniform is olive.

JEEP

LAVENDER

White and purple make lavender.
The bunny has lovely lavender eggs
in his basket.

LILACS

EASTER EGGS

RED   **YELLOW**   **BLUE**

Do you remember the names
of all these colors?
What is your favorite color?

I know colors.

Now you do, too!